MORTIMER

MORTIMER

STORY by
ROBERT MUNSCH

ART by
MICHAEL MARTCHENKO

annick press
toronto • berkeley

We acknowledge the support of the Canada Council for the Arts and the Ontario Arts Council, and the participation of the Government of Canada/la participation du gouvernement du Canada for our publishing activities.

ONTARIO ARTS COUNCIL
CONSEIL DES ARTS DE L'ONTARIO
an Ontario government agency
un organisme du gouvernement de l'Ontario

Library and Archives Canada Cataloguing in Publication

Munsch, Robert N., 1945-, author
      Mortimer / Robert Munsch ; [illustrations by] Michael Martchenko.

(Classic Munsch)
Previously published: Toronto : Annick Press, ©1983.
ISBN 978-1-77321-083-4 (hardcover).--ISBN 978-1-77321-082-7 (softcover)

      I. Martchenko, Michael, illustrator II. Title.

PS8576.U575M6 2018   jC813'.54   C2018-901422-9

Published in the U.S.A. by Annick Press (U.S.) Ltd.
Distributed in Canada by University of Toronto Press.
Distributed in the U.S.A. by Publishers Group West.

Printed in China.

www.annickpress.com
www.robertmunsch.com

Also available in e-book format. Please visit www.annickpress.com/ebooks.html for more details.

To Billy,
Sheila, and
Kathleen
Cronin

One night Mortimer's mother took him
upstairs to go to bed—

THUMP

THUMP

THUMP

THUMP

THUMP

THUMP.

When they got upstairs Mortimer's
mother opened the door to his room.

She threw him into bed and said,

"MORTIMER, BE QUIET."

Mortimer shook his head, yes.

The mother shut the door.
Then she went back down the stairs—

THUMP

    THUMP

        THUMP

            THUMP

                THUMP.

As soon as she got back downstairs
Mortimer sang,

Clang, clang, rattle-bing-bang
Gonna make my noise all day.
Clang, clang, rattle-bing-bang
Gonna make my noise all day.

Mortimer's father heard all that noise.
He came up the stairs—

 THUMP

THUMP

 THUMP

THUMP

THUMP

THUMP.

He opened the door and yelled,

"MORTIMER, BE QUIET."

Mortimer shook his head, yes.

The father went back down the stairs—

THUMP

THUMP

THUMP

THUMP

THUMP.

As soon as he got to the bottom of the stairs Mortimer sang,

Clang, clang, rattle-bing-bang
Gonna make my noise all day.
Clang, clang, rattle-bing-bang
Gonna make my noise all day.

All of Mortimer's seventeen brothers
and sisters heard that noise, and they
all came up the stairs—

THUMP

THUMP

THUMP

THUMP

THUMP

THUMP.

They opened the door and yelled in a
tremendous, loud voice,

"MORTIMER, BE QUIET."

Mortimer shook his head, yes.

The brothers and sisters shut the door
and went downstairs—

THUMP

    THUMP

        THUMP

            THUMP

                THUMP.

As soon as they got to the bottom of
the stairs Mortimer sang,

> *Clang, clang, rattle-bing-bang*
> *Gonna make my noise all day.*
> *Clang, clang, rattle-bing-bang*
> *Gonna make my noise all day.*

They got so upset that they called the police. Two policemen came and they walked very slowly up the stairs—

THUMP

THUMP

THUMP

THUMP

THUMP

THUMP.

They opened the door and said in very deep, policemen-type voices,

"MORTIMER, BE QUIET."

The policemen shut the door and went
back down the stairs—

THUMP

  THUMP

    THUMP

      THUMP

        THUMP.

As soon as they got to the bottom of
the stairs Mortimer sang,

Clang, clang, rattle-bing-bang
Gonna make my noise all day.
Clang, clang, rattle-bing-bang
Gonna make my noise all day.

Well, downstairs no one knew what to do.

The mother got into a big fight with the policemen.

The father got into a big fight with the brothers and sisters.

Upstairs, Mortimer got so tired waiting for someone to come up that he fell asleep.

Even More Classic Munsch:

Classic Munsch ABC
The Dark
Mud Puddle
The Paper Bag Princess
The Boy in the Drawer
Jonathan Cleaned Up—Then He Heard a Sound
Millicent and the Wind
Murmel, Murmel, Murmel
The Fire Station
Angela's Airplane
David's Father
Thomas' Snowsuit
50 Below Zero
I Have to Go!
Moira's Birthday
A Promise is a Promise
Pigs
Something Good
Show and Tell
Purple, Green and Yellow
Wait and See
Where is Gah-Ning?
From Far Away
Stephanie's Ponytail
Munschworks: The First Munsch Collection
Munschworks 2: The Second Munsch Treasury
Munschworks 3: The Third Munsch Treasury
Munschworks 4: The Fourth Munsch Treasury
The Munschworks Grand Treasury
Munsch Mini-Treasury One
Munsch Mini-Treasury Two
Munsch Mini-Treasury Three

For information on these titles please visit www.annickpress.com
Many Munsch titles are available in French and/or Spanish, as well as in
board book and e-book editions. Please contact your favorite supplier.